T0195951

The Angel Babies

Chapter.13.14.

CLIVE ALANDO TAYLOR

authorHOUSE

AuthorHouse™ UK
1663 Liberty Drive
Bloomington, IN 47403 USA
www.authorhouse.co.uk
Phone: 0800.197.4150

© 2019 Clive Alando Taylor. All rights reserved.

*No part of this book may be reproduced, stored in a retrieval system, or transmitted
by any means without the written permission of the author.*

Published by AuthorHouse 03/05/2019

ISBN: 978-1-7283-8555-6 (sc)
ISBN: 978-1-7283-8556-3 (e)

Print information available on the last page.

*Any people depicted in stock imagery provided by Getty Images are models,
and such images are being used for illustrative purposes only.
Certain stock imagery © Getty Images.*

This book is printed on acid-free paper.

*Because of the dynamic nature of the Internet, any web addresses or links contained in this book may have changed
since publication and may no longer be valid. The views expressed in this work are solely those of the author and do
not necessarily reflect the views of the publisher, and the publisher hereby disclaims any responsibility for them.*

Contents

Angelus Domini .13.14.

INSPIRIT*ASPIRE*ESPRIT*INSPIRE

Because of the things that have first become proclaimed within the spirit, and then translated in the soul, in order for the body to then become alive and responsive or to aspire, or to be inspired, if only then for the body to become a vessel, or a catalyst, or indeed an instrument of will, with which first the living spirit that gave life to it, along with the merits and the meaning of life, and the instruction and the interpretation of life, is simply to understand that the relationship between the spirit and the soul, are also the one living embodiment with which all things are one, and become connected and interwoven by creating, or causing what we can come to call, or refer to as the essence, or the cradle, or the fabric of life, which is in itself part physical and part spirit.

And so it is, that we are all brought in being, along with this primordial and spiritual birth, and along with this the presence or the origins of the spirit, which is also the fabric and the nurturer of the soul with which the body can be formed, albeit that by human standards, this act of nature however natural, can now take place through the act of procreation or consummation, and so it is with regard to this living spirit that we are also upon our natural and physical birth, given a name and a number, inasmuch that we represent, or become identified by a color, or upon our created formation and distinction of identity, we become recognized by our individuality.

But concerning the Angels, it has always been of an interest to me how their very conception, or existence, or origin from nature and imagination, could have become formed and brought into being, as overtime I have heard several stories of how with the event of the first creation of man, that upon this event, that all the Angels were made to accept and to serve in God's creation of man, and that man was permitted to give command to these Angels in the event of his life, and the trials of his life which were to be mastered, but within this godly decree and narrative, we also see that there was all but one Angel that either disagreed or disapproved with, not only the creation of man, but also with the formation of this covenant between God and man, and that all but one Angel was Satan, who was somewhat displeased with God's creation of man, and in by doing so would not succumb or show respect or demonstrate servility or humility toward man or mankind.

As overtime it was also revealed to me, that with the creation of the Angels, that it was also much to their advantage as it was to ours, for the Angels themselves to adhere to this role and to serve in the best interest of man's endeavors upon the face of the earth, as long as man himself could demonstrate and become of a will and a nature to practice his faith with a spirit, and a soul, and a body that would become attuned to a godly or godlike nature, and in by doing so, and in by believing so, that all of his needs would be met with accordingly.

And so this perspective brings me to question my own faith and ideas about the concept and the ideology of Angels, insomuch so that I needed to address and to explore my own minds revelation, and to investigate that which I was told or at least that which I thought I knew concerning the Angels along with the juxtaposition that if Satan along with those Angels opposed to serving God's creation of man, and of those that did indeed seek to serve and to favor God's creation and to meet with the merits, and the dreams, and the aspirations of man, that could indeed cause us all to be at the mercy and the subjection of an externally influential and internal spiritual struggle or spiritual warfare, not only with ourselves, but also with our primordial and spiritual identity.

And also because of our own conceptual reasoning and comprehension beyond this event, is that we almost find ourselves astonished into believing that this idea of rights over our mortal souls or being, must have begun or started long ago, or at least long before any of us were even souls inhabiting our physical bodies here as a living presence upon the face of the earth, and such is this constructed dilemma behind our beliefs or identities, or the fact that the names, or the numbers that we have all been given, or that have at least become assigned to us, is simply because of the fact that we have all been born into the physical world.

As even I in my attempts, to try to come to terms with the very idea of how nature and creation could allow so many of us to question this reason of totality, if only for me to present to you the story of the Angel Babies, if only to understand, or to restore if your faith along with mine, back into the realms of mankind and humanity, as I have also come to reflect in my own approach and understanding of this narrative between God and Satan and the Angels, that also in recognizing that they all have the power to influence and to subject us to, as well as to direct mankind and humanity, either to our best or worst possibilities, if only then to challenge our primordial spiritual origin within the confines of our own lifestyles, and practices and beliefs, as if in our own efforts and practices that we are all each and every one of us, in subjection or at least examples and products of both good and bad influences.

Which is also why, that in our spiritual nature, that we often call out to these heavenly and external Angelic forces to approach us, and to heal us, and to bless us spiritually, which is, or has to be made to become a necessity, especially when there is a humane need for us to call out for the assistance, and the welfare, and the benefit of our own souls, and our own bodies to be aided or administered too, or indeed for the proper gifts to be bestowed upon us, to empower us in such a way, that we can receive guidance and make affirmations through the proper will and conduct of a satisfactory lesson learnt albeit through this practical application and understanding, if only to attain spiritual and fruitful lives.

As it is simply by recognizing that we are, or at some point or another in our lives, have always somewhat been open, or subject to the interpretations of spiritual warfare by reason of definition, in that Satan's interpretation of creation is something somewhat of contempt, in that God should do away with, or even destroy creation, but as much as Satan can only prove to tempt, or to provoke God into this reckoning, it is only simply by inadvertently influencing the concepts, or the ideologies of man, that of which whom God has also created to be creators, that man through his trials of life could also be deemed to be seen in Satan's view, that somehow God had failed in this act of creation, and that Satan who is also just an Angel, could somehow convince God of ending creation, as Satan himself cannot, nor does not possess the power to stop or to end creation, which of course is only in the hands of the creator.

And so this brings me back to the Angels, and of those that are in favor of either serving, or saving mankind from his own end and destruction, albeit that we are caught up in a primordial spiritual fight, that we are all engaged in, or by reason of definition born into, and so it is only by our choices that we ultimately pay for our sacrifice, or believe in our rights to life, inasmuch that we are all lifted up to our greatest effort or design, if we can learn to demonstrate and to accept our humanity in a way that regards and reflects our greater desire or need, to be something more than what we choose to believe is only in the hands of God the creator or indeed a spirit in the sky.

Chapter .XIII.

The Chamber Of The Elect Few

Time is neither here or there, it is a time in between time as it is the beginning and yet the end of time. This is a story of the Alpha and the Omega, the first and the last, and yet as we enter into this revelation, we begin to witness the birth of the Angel Babies a time of heavenly conception when dying Angels gave birth to Angelic children who were born to represent the order of the new world. The names of these Angel Babies remained unknown but they carried the Seal of their fathers written on their foreheads, and in ail it totalled one hundred and forty four thousand Angels and this is the story of one of them.

Angelus Domini

INSPIRIT*ASPIRE*ESPRIT*INSPIRE

Chapter .XIII.

The Chamber of the Elect Few

I am free, I am free from the despair, and free from the dictates of turmoil, and free to follow and free to roam wherever so this truth, and this desire may take me, and yet of all the dreams that have transcended beyond the Moon and descended upon the Earthly realms, I am now free to become the sole beneficiary of such things as of yet unseen, and yet high above me in the other worlds, is the never ending eventful turnings of the wheels of the Ophanim, and the ever changing dynamics of a futuristic horizon, a star, yet to awaken, now arising with the birth of one whose conception emerges from out of the all encompassing dark matter, where upon a time, all things are forged by the hands of eternity, before the dying remnants give new life to new energies, for how else could these sentinels that cling to the bosom of heaven, now exploding into life begin again yet another unending journey, a journey that takes and shapes the destiny of the minds, and the hearts of those that are freed, and yet if not forced and willingly expelled and compelled to go out in the search of their own definitive task of fulfillment, and yet the dream of Manoo, is only but the hint of a whisper, now found to be ringing within the air, as heeded upon the ears of I Angelus E' Nocturnālis.

Upon the first visitation, came upon me, Angelus An'jela, from the Celestial Abode, in claiming forth, that the darkness could no longer be permitted to be the dictates of the Earth, as even She herself, had stated in knowing, that this was not the way or the natural state of things, if only in order to prevent what was to come, is it not true to say, that your will has been granted, Yay or Nay, yes my Sister, my will is now the way of the world, and are you not yet satisfied that everything has ceased because of this will, no my Sister, Heaven has not ceased because of my will, no well perhaps not, but the Earth has now become neglected and separated because of this dream, and yet whereupon can the other be found, if you choose not to unify it, the other! Yes the other, is not true that you are one in the same, Oh yes An'jela, but are not all things conceived in the dark, no! They are not Nocturnus, and you have dwelled in the darkness for far too long, and it was left answerable to me, to appeal to your senses, so who sent you, now you know it doesn't require such cause and effect for such responses to compel us into action, then it was not Him or Her, nay, it was not, I came simply because it is time, time! Time for what, do not speak so foolishly E' Nocturnus, you have had your way for much than is warranted, warrant! Am I to be arrested, if need be yes, but the Celeste have no power or influence over me, nay, that is true, but the Empyreans do, so if need be, I shall appeal to them to uproot you, but this Heaven is only respondent to itself, even as the Earth weeps and sleeps and dies, then am I not the only beneficial caretaker, the Earth does not belong to you Nocturnus, nay it does not, but neither does it belong to you also.

Out of all the things that matter, what do you suppose it matters the most, and of all those things that matter the most, out of whom is the most significant one above all does it matter more too, so you wish to speak in riddles Nocturnus, yes, why not, well as it now appears that your intend and require to hold us all in contempt while keeping the Earth hostage and in eternal darkness for all eternity, no! An'jela, wrong answer, then what is the answer, I'm afraid I cannot divulge such a riddle to an inferior Sentinel such as yourself, but let me hasten to add, that if one can answer such a riddle, then I shall redeem myself and reveal the other to you, is that not fair my Celeste, fair enough, then I shall find out such an answer and return again to speak and reveal the answer to you, so that the other might be released, that is all, yes my Sister, that is all, and with that a tiny flickering light vanished right before my eyes, almost blinding and blurring my vision, until once again I took some comfort, surrounded by the infinite depths of dark, but who or what is coming next, I know I cannot see you, but I know that you are out there somewhere, aren't you, but why exactly is the wind whispering Manoo.

Once upon a distant future, a girl child was saved from a dystopic cold and isolated world which found itself lost in the decaying nightmare of its' own advancement, brought forth unto the realms of the Empyreans to be raised as the Earth Mother Uama within the household of Selah, in bearing the child Manoo, of Angel Ruen, who's repatriation after his excommunication of the Angels of the Empyreans, was overseen and validated by Haven the newly elected Herald Angel, as a Tutee Savant, and specialist within the modern studies of the humanities, Manoo was always challenged in his thinking as to the decline and decimation of the recent past, and the lapse of humankind into such a tragedy of destruction, much of which was akin, due to the past histories of the world, that he one day wished and desired to address, if he and indeed the household of Selah were to return to reinhabit such a physical place again, as even in this present place, many scholars would sit and passionately debate the disgraceful fate of the Earth, inasmuch that it should not be revived due to the ideas and thinking, that inevitably it would only serve to reap the same repeatable consequences that had already come to pass, but Manoo did not believe or see it this way, as his defense was not too dissimilar from the prophets of old who had also warned of God's wrath, carried forth and exacted upon the world, except that Manoo within his modern thinking, would defend that this wrath however fulfilled was not to be treated or seen as finite, in that God would not enact the same thing twice, but instead renew his agreement with anyone worthy or mad enough to carry this promise forward, and yet none amongst them was willing or even prepared enough to take on such a task, as the thought of failure or disappointment, or the sheer magnitude that God, who would always single out one soul from amongst the multitude to fulfill such a task, and yet as it stood, all who feared God, also feared this burden.

The Earth is no more, and so who are we the elect few to resurrect it, if the Earth has been judged and found diminished to be an unfit place, then why should we waste time upon our time of deliberations to consider it, let it be as it has already been done, and if the Messiah has already passed over the Earth, then has not thy will been done, yes it is true my fellow elect, but thy will has not been done on Earth, as it is in Heaven, but give us this Day, which Day Manoo! Which day when these days are no more, Haven is our sanctuary now, yes, yes I know, but did you not see that even mine own father had also become redeemed and saved from the nothingness that befalls upon the forgotten, so what of the Earth now, can she not also be brought back into the alignment of these Heavens, nay Manoo, it is not so, we have reached the point of no return, as it was written that upon the Dawn of the Rubicon, that we loosened our grip, as we let the Devil slip, falling straight into a world of utter confusion, yes my fellows, but who commands this Rubicon, or did you not overlook it before you sat down and heeded the instructions, and when you reached the end did you not comprehend and conclude that it only led to our destruction, and yet after the night comes the dawn, so why are we to be afraid of predictions, if the Seal is broken and left open, then is there not an opportunity for all things to be made possible, as there may still be time to afford and reap the rewards of a parable full of talents, or should we just idly sit by and say and do nothing to salvage this place, then let me address this counsel in asking what is your true purpose, if only to live and dwell upon the past, Manoo this is not true, except to say that you are truly a madman of no descript, well all I can say my fellow elect in response to your short sighted idleness, is that it is you who are simply foolish, thoughtless in your sanctimonious ways.

As the debate continued, a Celestial approached the threshold of the Empyreans, what is presence here Celeste, I have come in seeking after the one, Haven the Herald Angel, for what purpose do you come to seek counsel with Haven, O' Gatekeeper, it is a matter of the most urgency, for the gravity of the Earth is heavily weighted in darkness and affects the very pillars that support it, very well then, enter therein and momentarily Haven will appear before you, as Angelus An'jela had entered into the midst of the Empyreans, she was instantly mesmerized by the complex beauty of this place, as it stretched far and wide, with each strand of this Cosmos extending high and low, like branches of a thriving, living tree of life, extending itself beyond the expanse, touching and encompassing every star arising, as it was in that moment of awe and bewilderment that Haven did now appear before An'jela.

My Herald, I have heard of you and your legacy and your many trials of challenges and triumphs, yes my Celeste, but all glory is always due to God, yes my Herald all such glory is justly so, but permit me if I may inquire to ask, but how is it, that the Earth has been made to become cut off from the rest of the Heavens, in causing such imbalances to affect those critical structures that were once crafted and made perfect for the harmony of all things to take nurture and flourish, surely the Earth cannot be held and kept in limbo for all eternity, yes my Celeste, it is true to say that this period of darkness has continued for much too long, but it was prophesied by the ancient ones that such a time and period would envelope the Earth up until such a time, that God would restore a new Heaven and a new Earth, yes my Herald, but this time of prediction has no end, for when will it be that such a period will come to pass, or will another season come and go before God is impassioned to move Heaven and Earth once again, my Celeste, I am touches by your cries of despair, but the time has not yet expired for the Earth to become renewed, then when is this time my Herald, as Nocturnus has become defiled and corrupt and is coveting this place as his own, he is also meddlesome and interferes with the natural order of things, yes my Celeste, I am also aware of the two sided nature of Angelus E' Nocturnus, but he has been appointed there for that very reason, as a generation has now come to pass since Nocturnus too upon himself this role, but you are right, he has become like a demon, where the light has diminished, except that he also holds the key to the other, so we must attempt to appease him into revealing this concealment, yes I have tried, but as for now he only speaks in riddles, riddles! Yes my Herald, I believe that Angelus E' Nocturnālis, has forgotten himself due to the darkness that has consumed his very nature, so the other is hidden or perhaps buried.

So you mean to say that Nocturnus has forgotten the other side, yes my Herald, the light is gone, and we have no means to retrieve it from his angelic mind, as it is the other the one who is lost to it, Oh I see, so perhaps the time has come to address this matter, yes my Herald, the time is now, or the opportunity will become lost to us forever, he has spoken of a riddle, that if answered correctly, would reveal the other and set E'

Nocturnus free from the darkness, so why not inquire after the wisest of such scholars, of whom can solve to answer such mysterious questions, very well, I shall approach those amongst the elect few, who often debate such matters on these subjects, who are these elect few, they are gifted philosophers, and have acquired substantial knowledge under the tutorials of the Ages, who have nurtured and taught the generations their own history concerning Heaven and Earth, good, I should like to be introduced into the presence of these elect few.

During the debate upon the future of the Earth, the Earth Mother Uama had entered into their presence in order to spend some time with her beloved Son Manoo, if you excuse me Elected Ones, but I believe that this conversation may carry on day after day, but for now you shall postpone toing and froing, as time is one precious commodity that we must not squander, but the Earth is being called into question Mother, yes Manoo, but that subject is now a distant memory relegated to the past, yes but how can you say that when it is your natural home and birthplace, yes, it true to say, that I was born there, but I grew up in Heaven, as so too did you, for if I was not saved, then you too would not have been born, yes I understand that, but my Father did this for a selfish reason, for himself, to save himself from the past misdeeds of his own reckless behavior, as even he desired to see the end of world, from the origins of the bowl judgments, no Manoo, he did what was required of Heaven, so that we could have peace and harmony and a life of living abundance, and you are not so simple and ordinary my son, as you have the Empyrean blood coursing through your veins, as I am sure one day that you shall rise to great prominence, but I should suggest that you take this time to look away from the world, and instead focus your thoughts and energies upon the generations such as yourself, now being presented with the dreams that we could not fathom or even begin to realize, but that's it Mother, the dream is being realized, and it points to and indicates to me, that the Earth must abundantly flourish once again.

Mother Uama, whether or not it is the past, how can we know the future if we don't examine where we once came from, of all the awakened and enlightened minds, why is there so much negative discourse surrounding the Earth, my Son, it is because with the history of the world, that we are left with no choice other than to abandon it, for it will always become a playground for demons and devils alike, of course great men and women have arisen out of its' womb, and yet all attempts have still failed to find the common grace and good now found to be associated with the same outcome resulting in corruptible power, whether it be, traditionalist or reformer, liberalist or conservatism, revolutionist or ideological, as all man's methods have tried and yet failed to arrive at a time, when they could see the world it was intended, and yet all were permitted and allowed to be played out instrumentally towards the fullness of its' own conclusive finality, and so now every soul is reluctant to attempt to fulfill such a promise as intended, now let us tie up this debate and put this subject to rest, but what of pioneers and innovators, and creationists and visionaries, and what of dreamers and geniuses, have they also failed in their attempts to fulfill this intended promise, Manoo! I know your heart and mind are born of riches filled with wonder, but we cannot change what has already been.

As Manoo and his Mother, were continuing to have their discussion, Haven the Herald Angel and An'jela of the Celestial Abode, entered into their company, My Herald, tell me what brings you here into the chamber of the Elect Few, I have come to associate you with a visitor, yes of course the Celeste is most welcome here, but of what matters are we to be concerned with, the matter is one of the Earth, and the light of the world, yes' yes my Celeste now please continue, as this is the very subject that we are all concerned with at this very moment in time, well as you are aware that the darkness that surrounds Her, has now begun to affect every aspect of space, gravity, and the elements that sustain and balance all other properties and energies, as I have also seen firsthand how the Angelus E' Nocturnālis has been allowed to be become freed, bringing about the desecration of the dying Earth, which has been allowed to go unchecked for such a long period of time, that I now believe, that if this neglect is to be prolonged any longer, then the effects of these seeds, could spread even further and wider, other than just being contained within this one sphere alone, as it could even permeate and manifest unto these Heavens, as much as we have already become aware of this within the Celestial Abode.

So you believe that the immediate Heavens are threatened in becoming affected by the cancerous seeds of darkness, yes this what I believe, then we must act quickly in response to this potential threat, nay we do not agree, the Earth is now finished, done away with and at long last forgotten, Her dying decaying form cannot change or even affect the Heavens, this is a most ridiculous notion that should not be heeded or even entertained, but don't you see my fellow Savants that Nocturnus has failed in his duty as the Earths caretaker to manage these dark elements, that even now the Earth has begun to manifest like an infected wound in need of healing, otherwise we may have to contend with another problem of containing Nocturnus himself, yes my Savant, but this not so simple, as Nocturnus is a complicated Angel, in that he also conceals the other, the other, tell me Celeste, what is the other, allow me to explain Manoo, yes my Herald please explain.

As you may not all be aware, but every Angel has a unique and individualistic talent, in that we all contain a special and gifted element embedded within us from our creator, but as for Angelus E' Nocturnālis, well he is not just simply the caretaker of the darkness now being inflicted upon the Earth, but he is, or should I say also contains the element of Light, otherwise known as Angelus E' Diurnal, but how is that even possible, well for whatever purpose of creation, perhaps God saw it befitting to put and place both light and dark within one embodiment, and so that is why An'jela is referring to it as the other, the other in this case, is Angelus E' Diurnāl, except that for now E' Nocturnus is the most prominent and dominant factor or presence that we may have to contend with, so what you are saying is that we have to somehow separate light from dark as constituted within the embodiment of one Angel, yes! That's exactly it, but there may be another way to awaken the other, and what way is that, well if it may be possible to provide an answer to this riddle, and what is this riddle my Celeste, well he spoke in saying, "Out of all the things that matter, what do you suppose it matters the most, and of all those things that matter the most, out of whom is the most significant one above all does it matter more too", have you ever heard of such profound statement before Manoo, no I can't say I have, but I shall consider it, but of course it does seems to suggest the most illogical superiority of what is more important above all, and which one of us holds more importance above the other, but isn't that love, well perhaps, or perhaps not, as the riddle itself is nonsensical, so perhaps we need to look at it more closely.

Perhaps we may approach the Hayyoth, who may be of some help in acquiring such an answer to this riddle, the Hayyoth, but what manner of beings are these my Herald, they are the four Angels of the Merkabah, who guide mystics upon the tours of Heaven, I have heard of these Angels, but is it not frightful to gaze upon them my Herald, nay, do not be fearful of them, for they are loyal and steadfast, and only ever to seek to watch over every proceeding in giving thanks and worship around the presence of Ophanim, then let us approach and inquire after them, well I'm afraid that this is not possible for you Manoo or even you An'jela, as you must in possession of the Angelic Aura, but I thought that they also toured Heaven, so tell us when are they due to descend upon us again, yes that is unless I go in place of you to pose the riddle and then return with the answer, then let it be so Haven, as we shall remain and dwell here and await upon your response.

As Haven the Herald Angel departed company from Manoo son of the Earth Mother Uama, and the Angel of the Celestial Abode An'jela, he was now able to reflect upon and anticipate his journey, as upon previous occasions, when he had experienced and witnessed the power of God through his Archangels and the mystery of the interchangeable Wheels set upon the Throne that influenced the turning of the Ophanim, do you think he that he will return with the answer, yes! Of course he will, he has

7

too, so that we can finally defeat Nocturnus and reveal the light of E' Diurnāl, yes but even if we reveal this light, won't it just result in one extreme after another, as surely we can't allow for the world to go from complete darkness into complete light, as we need to strike a balance between the both, yes you are right, but how is it even possible to divide one from the other, well perhaps the Hayyoth may also provide us with the answers that we need to these questions, upon reaching the Sea of Glass, Haven stopped within his ascent, to look and gaze upon the place where once Haven and Zyxven, were also just like E' Nocturnus and E' Diurnāl, in being one of the same heavenly body.

As he ascended even higher and further towards the Ophanim, where time seemingly appeared to be suspended, as a light and then four spirits, and a divine body appeared, as the Merkabah presented itself before Haven, emitting spirals of energy, now becoming connected and in tune with the higher realms of his own consciousness, and yet even before the Herald Angel could summons the Hayyoth, they appeared as one unified voice, and simply transmitted their message, observe, as it was upon that remark, that naturally as it expired, that Haven was somewhat compelled to speak sparingly in only being permitted to say what was necessary, "Out of all the things that matter, what do you suppose it matters the most" "And of all those things that matter the most, out of whom is the most significant one above all does it matter more too", as it was also upon their guarded response of austerity from the Merkabah, that the Hayyoth replied in saying, "Surrender to us the eyes of the night, for it transports the spirit and the body from one dimension to another, God and the Earth", and with that statement, the light faded away, and the four spirits disappeared, and the Merkabah vanished from sight, and so once again Haven was left to descend back towards the Empyreans.

Upon his return, Haven descended to the place of the Chamber of the Elect Few, where Manoo and An'jela along with Uama were waiting, I have seen the Hayyoth, and they have spoken to me in such a measured terms, that I only fear that I may have even complicated the riddle of E' Nocturnus even further, but what was it that they spoke and revealed to you, quite profoundly they said "Surrender to us the eyes of the night, for it transports the spirit and the body from one dimension to another, God and the Earth" but are you sure that you delivered the riddle correctly Haven, yes of course, of that much I am sure, then it seems the riddle has been answered with yet but another riddle, but what does this mean, and what or where are the eyes of the night.

Permit me if I may say something, yes Mother Uama, tell us, what is it, well perhaps the eyes, that the Hayyoth have demanded, are the eyes of Nocturnus himself, go on, and perhaps the things that matter, are only lightness and darkness, and yet it only matters the most to those who do not yet possess it, go on, go on, and so of all those things that matter the most must be the Earth, and the most significant one above all it matters too more, is God, yes, you have it, you have solved the riddle, but what if the answer is wrong, no! We must trust that this is answer to the riddle, as it is the only feasible one to contend with, but what of the eyes, how are we to remove the eyes of Nocturnus, my Father, my Father is the only one to do it, but Manoo, your Father is now redeemed and free from the trials of such arduous and burdensome tasks, then who else can endure in battle with E' Nocturnus, I can, but you are no match for him An'jela, yes but if you assist to distract him Manoo, then perhaps it will give me the chance to remove his eyes, very well then, you must grant me safe passage to the Earth, and we shall attempt to defy Nocturnus together if he is not willing to yield to the submission of our agreement if we answer the riddle correctly, good, then it is agreed, come let us go now, but are you sure this is the way An'jela, yes Haven, it is the only way, I shall accompany Manoo, and we shall face Nocturnus together, very well then, Godspeed, please Manoo do not be foolish my Son, this is madness, yes Mother I know, but unfortunately it must be done, thy will must be done Mother Uama, then go, go and bring light to the world if you can, as you have my blessing.

At last my Celeste, I shall descend from the Empyreans and place my feet upon the Earth, the natural home and habitat of my forbearers, and of those who came before me, my ancestors, pay heed and listen well young Manoo, and watch as you should only walk in the ways that I walk, for the Earth is darkened and full of traps and snares that may cause you harm, as I shall take you to the places where you have never been, but remember that you in particular Manoo do not come from Earth, as your origins have always come from Heaven first and foremost, even though you may have a spiritual inclination towards it, as does any child conceived in Heaven, but firstly you must learn to walk in the ways of God, in order to ensure that the ground beneath your feet is made firm and strong enough, and worthy to be walked upon, upright straight and noble, Manoo, Manoo, yes Manoo walks with God, yes my Celeste, my path is made steady, and the ground below my feet are secured safely in order not to stumble in the ways that you have guided me, then come, let us descend below, and so An'jela took Manoo by the hand, and led him first through the threshold and across the breadth and the width of the heavens, and then gently they glided down toward the Earth below.

As they both entered into the earth's stratosphere, and instantly the thin air became cold and freezing, and yet the sky beneath them was blackened and blotted out, without any light that could penetrate it, and yet the air below was thick and stuffy and somewhat stifling and suffocating, making it difficult to breathe, is this the Earth my Celeste, yes Manoo this is it, but it was not always like this, then what has happened to it, where are the living creatures that once inhabited it, they are no more Manoo, but I have heard many stories about rivers flowing, streaming down from the mountains into the seas, and of the birds that fly and soar high above into the sky, and of the wild animals that roam across the untamed expanses, and of all the things that live and abide by the forest and trees, but where are they now, they are also no more Manoo, but why has God allowed this to happen my Celeste, I do not know why Manoo, except that perhaps he or she has chosen not to prevent it, then for what bargaining or profit is Nocturnus allowed to have such principality over all of this, if there was another way Manoo, then I do not know it, except that the darkness is spreading even further now, and threatens to consume and poison everything in its' path, as once it was that the union of Heaven and Earth were intrinsically tied together for our continued relationship, but as for now, She has become cut off.

The smell and the stench of decay was in the air as they approached and drew near to the places that Angelus E' Nocturnālis frequented, as this spawned Angel had now embedded and manifested himself within the lair and the crust of the Earth, I see that you have returned my Celeste with company in tow, yes Nocturnus, so tell me who is this newly accompanying stranger that you have brought with you, my name is Manoo, Manoo, a strange and yet familiar name that you speak, and what manner of a name and specimen is Manoo, his name means walks with God, God! Walk! Is that it, do you mean to tell me that he only walks and cannot fly, nay I cannot, but that's absurd, I was expecting an Angel of the Empyreans, to engage with me and to entertain me, not a mere boy who can only walk, we have come to reveal the answer to your riddle Nocturnus, so that we might reveal the other, and cause the light to breakout across the Earth, O' have you now, and what do you know of the other, we know that he lives and breathes beside you in his stead, O' very good my Celeste, so the answer to the riddle, but I have already forgotten about that, why not let us begin with a new riddle, something that Master Manoo, can possibly decipher, but we already have an agreement, yes, yes, I know but I don't recall it so, do not promote utter nonsense and idiosyncrasies in toying with me Angelus, but I relish the company my Celeste as no one ever comes to see me anymore, to spend time with me, if only to ponder such useless pastimes, stop it Angelus, and let her deliver the answer to the riddle, yes' yes' Manoo, but the question remains, do you know the answer to this riddle, and permit me if I may ask, but was it you who solved it, nay it was not, it was my Mother, the Earth Mother Uama.

Your Mother, yes my Mother Uama, and how did she come to solve this riddle, my Mother is wise in her years, as she was once a child of the Earth, yes a child of the Earth, I have heard of this child, the last one saved from the wrath of God, taken up into Heaven by Angel Ruen, the angelic descendant of the now disgraced Ophlyn, now relegated to the forgotten annals of Pablo' accounts and safekeeping of the unwritten laws, so am I right in assuming that Manoo is the angelic offspring of Ruen also, yes my Father is Angel Ruen, Ruen! And yet no wings, a slight reductive demotion perhaps for his past misdeeds, my Father has always done what was required of him, yes Manoo, yes as we are all required to do what is necessary, but I would just simply like to know who my adversaries are both inside and out, now to the question and toward the task at hand, the riddle.

For just for one second Nocturnus's voice changed as his eyes went from Scarlet to Gold and then back again, as if something deep within him had shifted or revived in him, yes now where was I, O' yes so once again, if the eyes are the window to the soul, which one is Scarlet and which one is Gold, but that's not the riddle, O' but it is young Manoo son of Ruen, but what does Scarlet and Gold have to do with the eyes being the window of the soul, day and night perhaps, light and dark, inside out, O' I see, one of you are the other, and one of you are not, yes, yes, very good Manoo, now which one of you shall pose to answer the riddle, An'jela perhaps you, no! Let Manoo answer it, very well then Manoo,

I shall prepare to repeat myself, out of all the things that matter, what do you suppose it matters the most, and of all those things that matter the most, out of whom is the most significant one above all does it matter more too.

"Out of all the things that matter, what do you suppose it matters the most" "The things that matter, are only lightness and darkness, and yet it only matters the most to those who do not yet possess it", "And of all those things that matter the most, out of whom is the most significant one above all does it matter more too", Of all those things that matter the most, is the Earth, and the most significant one above all it matters too more, is God, very good Manoo, very good indeed, but I'm afraid that I cannot accept your answer, but why not, because the question was answered by your Mother and not the Angel Celeste An'jela, of whom the question was first posed too, but that was the right answer wasn't it, Yes! But that's not fair Nocturnus, and who said it would be fair, as neither you, nor l, or God knows nothing of fairness, but we have answered the riddle correctly, nay as it is in my power to reject it, because my Celeste could not and did not answer it directly herself.

Just then An'jela became enraged, you are a deceiver and a cheat Nocturnus, and you my Celeste are a sore loser, but you tricked us Angelus, yes I did, but then again no I did not, then allow me to pose a simple question Angelus, and what question is that Manoo, well I would like to ask it of the other, O' you would now would you, yes I would, just then Nocturnus became silent, and began to react nervously and erratically, as if becoming uncomfortable and irritated within his own skin, as if at odds with some kind of internal power struggle taking place inside of him, or at least as if a conflict of interest was now being fought between two individual or separate personalities, and so Manoo continued to insist, E' Diurnāl, if you can hear me then speak, as I wish to pose a question to you, the other, please answer me or show me a sign, just then Nocturnus's eyes began to glow, from Scarlet to Gold, and then from Gold to Scarlet as Manoo looked on, its' happening now An'jela, yes it is, I can see that, but which one and when should I pluck, I'm not sure, but Scarlet is more often than not associated with darkness, so do it when they are red and not before, as Nocturnus fought to keep E' Diurnāl at bay, his eyes kept changing color back and forth between the two shades, can you hear me Angelus E' Diurnāl, can you hear me, please show us a sign, No! I will not allow you to break and divide me, I am Angelus E' Nocturnus, but just then as Nocturnus became conflicted within himself, his eyes began to glow like blood red scarlet, do it now An'jela, do it now, and so it was at this point that the Angel An'jela leapt forward and reached out in snatching both of his eyes from out of his head.

No sooner than An'jela the Celeste had plucked the eyes from Angelus E' Nocturnālis, that a transformation began to take shape and effect, as natural his form started to separate and divide itself, as if two cells were being caused to split from one another, as within that moment the angel Angelus E' Diurnāl began to emerge from the insides of Nocturnus, who was by now stepping out of the shadow this concealed angelic embodiment, in becoming released and revealing his own independent form and body, as if by some unique and supreme force that had enveloped these two deities was broken, as the now freely emancipated E' Diurnāl stood before them, with the somewhat astonished An'jela and Manoo, who now bore witness to not one but two miraculous individual Angels, of which one who stood with eyes of Gold, and the other now blinded by his own arrogance and insolence, as it was during this metamorphosis, that the heavens began to thunder loudly, striking against the blackened sky as flashes of lightning leapt forward, as, Nocturnus screamed out in defiance! Give me back my eyes.

You may think that you have defeated me don't you, but as of yet you fail to grasp the meaning behind your actions, as I was forged in the darkness, much like the creation of man itself, as I am the muse of darkness, as within the tone of his torment, Nocturnus dropped down to his knees and dipped his hands into the sodden Earth, whilst grabbing the earthly clay and mud and began by shaping and molding it into the sockets of his eyes, as if he could somehow salvage his ability to restore and heal his sight from using the mud and clay that he was now clinging too, as An'jela and Manoo looked on in shock and desperation, as the newly liberated E' Diurnāl came before them in saying, "Light is born, and the darkness cannot triumph over me any longer, Yes it is, but darkness is formed and can neither be defeated or eliminated, and so a battle had now begun, as Nocturnus, who by now could only the ability to make out the shapes and outline of objects in his attempts to strike out at the Angelus E' Diurnāl, as they began their external and infinite power struggle.

An'jela stepped back in shock and horror, fearfully grabbing hold of Manoo, what have I done, what have we unleashed here this day upon the Earth, as the two Angels took to the skies, exchanging blow after blow upon each other, inflicting the severest of punishment, with one upon the other, I cannot be kept in eternal darkness, and I cannot be submissive to eternal light, then one of us must die, nay for the darkness must come out of the light, nay the darkness has covered the yellow Sun for far too long, forgive me for my absoluteness my friend and nemesis, but aren't you forgetting that in the beginning, it was the earth that was covered in darkness, yes but with the exception, this is not the beginning, as the madness of the battle endured and continued, An'jela, became afraid that this struggle would remain forever never ending with no true triumphant victor of one overcoming the other, and so Manoo, who thought of nothing else to do, coupled and pressed his hands together and began to pray.

Now this was no simple or ordinary prayer of invocation, as it ascended upwardly as it tore through the very essence and fabric of Heaven itself, and yet as it rippled its' way through into the universal cosmos of the stars, this was a prayer of lineage and legacy, of history and ancestry, as much as it was a prayer of hereditary empyrean blood, and so as it passed from Manoo and through into the spirit of Ruen, and yet even deeper and further still, now surpassing and submitting itself unto the mysteries beyond the annals of the unwritten laws, until lastly and eventually, it came to land at the feet of none other than that of Ophlyn himself, as if this beginning of an imminent rebirth had become reignited, for the way and the path to be made clear for Angel Ophlyn to arise out of the rapturous thunder, and so instantly to appear before all who would dare to come and to seek out in summoning him.

As an Angel of the old order did appear before them like a shining sentinel, striking against the sky, and in announcing in a mightily and heavenly echoing voice, that set about to quake the ground below, "Be warned, Niphlegah! If day be night and night be day, then let them be set asunder, For of those whom God hath joined together, let them now be set apart", and with that prophetic saying, Angelus E' Nocturnālis, Angelus E' Diurnāl were once and for all separated and set apart and divided, and placed beyond the fathomless reach of one another, as An'jela and Manoo, who now stood to his feet, looked on with amazement and bewilderment, upon this awesome wonder of majestic sight, as he simply uttered the words "Grandfather" which was met with an affectionate smile moments before he dematerialized and disappeared, only in saying "Grand Ophlyn" and then he was gone, and seen no more.

Upon Ophlyn's mystical disappearance, everything fell silent, as an eerie misty reddish dust cloud began to rise up and glow, causing the first stages of light to filter and breakthrough the darkest stages of an astronomical twilight, now forming a huge haze across the Sky, as they both stood and looked on, now beginning to feel the first drops of water, as a deluge of rain started to fall, signaling the healing and the cleansing of the Earth, come Manoo it is time, let us take to flight and return back to the Empyreans, as the first clouds burst forth in issuing their rainwater to pour down upon the Earth beneath, and so it was that the Angel Celeste An'jela took Manoo by the hand and led him back through the stratosphere, and towards his angelic home, the Empyreans.

New friendships and relationships are formed every day, especially when we least expect it, and also bringing with it, new hopes and aspirations, and yet in such a little short space of time, both tragic and pleasant circumstances can create unbreakable bonds when we least expect them too, as such was the eventful experience and succession between our two hero's and heroine, that caused an infinity to affectionately develop between, as it was nothing other than fate that had flung them together and sealed and cemented such an unending bond, a bond that would prove itself to be of a shared and reciprocal feeling now becoming sincerely felt and truly realized between the Angel An'jela of the Celestial Abode, and that of Manoo, Son of Angel Ruen and the Earth Mother Uama, as once they had arrived upon the place of his birthing, they were immediately welcomed by all concerned of their trial and plight upon the Adama of the Earth, as Haven the Herald Angel and the Chamber of the Elect Few, gathered round to greet and receive them warmly and safely back into the bosom of Heaven.

As the word of their story was met with eager anticipation, as this eventful challenge was revealed, albeit with one exception, in that Manoo did not wish or desire to reveal that his grandfather for some strange reason had appeared before them at such an imminent and vital hour, but instead, that they had overcome E' Nocturnus by some other divine means, for he now felt in his heart, that somehow this revelation of the Grand Ophlyn, would or could somehow cause a manner of disturbances and suspicions, if indeed it became rumored that his spirit had somehow manifested more so, in becoming an even much more stronger and enduring force or potent omnipresence, and so the eyes of the night were handed to Haven, who once again began his ascent into the higher realms of the heavens to present himself before the Merkabah, in coming before the four creatures of the Hayyoth, whereupon he surrendered the eyes of Nocturnus into their safekeeping, as they in turn simply embellished and fashionably adorned it upon themselves, like a newly acquired ornamental jewel of objects, now becoming outwardly displayed upon their majestic and magnificent being, and placed along, with all the other eyes of divinity that overtime had come into their possession, and yet not once did Haven question or wonder, for what manner or purpose the importance of these eyes were to such creatures of mystery and mysticism, but instead acknowledged and revered at their divine obedience of loyalty to the spirit of the Ophanim.

For some strange and peculiar reason or even feeling, it had by now began to play upon Haven's mind, as to why such creatures would uphold such a dedicated commitment of unwavering devotion as displayed by the Hayyoth, forever defined by the homage, forever honoring a faithful command, set against the backdrop of a distant and yet familiar world now in decay and turmoil, or even why even this world, created by the hands of God, and yet warred upon by the histories and successions of Man, saved by the blood of his Son, that puzzled him the most, as to why would any such God, bring to life such a diverse and living creation, forever destined to evolve through an unending struggle of futility set against the trials of good over evil, in that any disobedience of defiance, would be met with a demerit of judgment, or even why such faithfulness, put beyond any reasonable doubt, would be deemed necessary upon all fronts, if not for every action of account to be met with in accordance with nothing else other than the purest and sincerest of acts and intentions, as no Man, and no Beast, and no Angel, could ever yet begin to grasp, or even overcome to begin to unfathom the unfathomable sovereign motives of God, or for what purpose was this intended complex world to be given, or to be saved or even handed over too.

Once upon a time there was a rumor or perhaps even a testament that supports the strangest theory of an account, of when a woman who became quite hysterical and overcome by the power of the Holy Spirit, when upon that fateful moment leading up to his crucifixion, whereupon she managed to push and force her way through the people who gathered in spectacle to watch as the messiah carried the cross towards an as of then unexplainable event, as she reached out from the busying hustle and bustle of the then crowd of onlookers, and then reached out her hand in adoring frustration, and stretched forth her hand in the vain hope of somehow touching the then Christ, but then only somehow, only succeeding in touching the hem of the cloth now adorned and draped across his beaten and battered body, as it was, that upon this one singular act of touching the shroud of Christ, that she shrieked out uncontrollably, and in professing madly, "I touched the hem of his cloth, I touched the hem of his cloth" and yet what does it mean to the savior amongst the saved, if not to be in his presence and be overcome by his spirit, and yet to only touch the hem of his cloth, then surely if there is truly power in the presence of Christ, and yet even more divine euphoria to feel his garment, then to what degree of measure does it multiply to become saved by his sacrificial blood, as every Angel in Heaven must acknowledge that this is the risen Christ.

Upon his return to the Empyreans, Haven sought to seek out An'jela, within the curiosities of his own account of seeing the Hayyoth, as they were all still sat within the Chamber, and in approaching the Celeste, he simply asked her, for what reason and purpose did you enter the Earth in seeking after Angelus E' Nocturnus, as I have said, it is because of the darkness that was too unbearable, as it was to begin along a path that was to consume everything, but tell me Celeste, when you first came upon him, what was he doing or saying, of that much I am not so sure, except I do believe that quite simply, he was praying, praying! Yes my Herald, he was quite literally praying, but to whom I do not know, except that he said, I am freed, or perhaps upon interpretation, I believe that he meant to say the truth had set himself free, but why, I do not know why my Herald, but for some strange and peculiar fashion, perhaps we have all asked ourselves why, and yet to no avail could this question be answered, which I must hasten to add, is also a puzzle and a riddle to us all.

As of when the Chamber of the Elect Few did begin to resume their debate, there was very little to surmise upon, in that the elected few, were somehow unprepared of how to issue forth any edicts concerning of how they should proceed forward upon the subject matters raised concerning the Earth, as it was more importantly a discussion of time versus miracles, as a well as a question of divine intervention, on how the Angels would set about fulfilling such a decree, or even how an age old prophecy would come to be fulfilled, in that upon the last days, there would indeed be a resurrected New Earth and more importantly a New Heaven, and yet my fellow Sentinels, is it not in God's holy divine power to instantly transform anything, yes it is, but as for this question of Man, Woman and Child, and of Fish and Mammal to flourish and inhabit the Earth once more, then are they not to become new beings and new creations of their former selves, and yet how can we be sure in our own divine abilities and expectations, that time after time, that they would not rely upon the miracles of Heaven to fulfill their every duty and command, as is not life built upon the statutes of day by day and trial by trial progresses, or are we not to be found independent of such revived reinventions.

Yes it is true to say that through such divinities of will, that the world below and above us can effortlessly become transformed overnight, but even he that professes to know the mind of God, knows not of how or when such divinity of motion is deemed necessary, or even sanctioned worthy in order to fulfill a greater ambition, as the way of this will is determined, not by its' exact and imminent immediacy, but is slow in its' maturing, and steady in its' progress, and timely in its' pursuits, and progressive within its' outcomes of deliverance, and yet as miraculous as miracles may seem, they would not be seen as such, or even become so rewarding or fulfilling, if indeed they happened and occurred upon every whim of cause and effect, unlest we accept that the most significant and ultimate, and effective ways and means, especially when faced with no other alternatives or outcomes, should we then begin to seek the assurances and the needs of such divinities of time to become enacted upon in such a phenomenal and supernatural way, as we must adhere to this commandment in order not to tempt or provoke such a will needlessly, and then somehow find ourselves in a contemptuous act of benile inactivity, but to do nothing is not necessarily to imply that we wait unprepared for any act or will to determined by the most high.

As the debate continued concerning the plans of the Earth and the time to come, Haven still remained somewhat troubled and doubtful about the account that An'jela the Celeste had revealed to him, and so he excused himself to in order conduct his own examination of the true reasons behind Angelus E' Nocturnus's prayer of freedoms as conveyed to him through the Celeste, and so to make himself scarce in becoming absent, he descended upon the Earth in the hope of seeking out this perplexing and riddled Angel, if only to learn the true nature of his intentions, and what may lay at the heart of his deliberate thinking and actions, as he would not have to wait too long before the Angelus E' Nocturnālis would reappear somewhat distressed and vexed by his ordeal.

I knew someone would come, but not you, not the Herald, I was rather thinking that perhaps Ruen would come to finish me off, nay Nocturnus, since becoming a Father, Angel Ruen is not the same, then why you, why have you come and not him, I have come because I am curious, as to why you would pray to keep the world in such darkness, why, why, everyone wants to know why, but tell me something Haven, the Herald, do you believe that somehow the darkness is evil, what do you mean, I mean what I say Herald, do you believe that darkness equates evil, well no, not if you put it like that, exactly, and did you know that in the context of Heaven and Earth, that the Heaven is depicted as light, and the Earth is depicted as dark, yes I see but, no, no buts, the Earth is as I have said, but with one exception, well what exception is that, it is my friend, the difference between Golgotha and Calvary, go on.

It does not take a fool to comprehend and admit to himself that darkness and light cannot become separated, for where there is darkness there is light, do you agree, yes I agree, but does this have to do with Golgotha and Calvary, it has everything to do with it, on one side of darkness is Golgotha, and on the other side is light, the light of Calvary, and yet in the middle what do we find, go on, we find the Messiah, yes but, no, no buts, let me explain, as there are also two elements of light involved, go on, one is the bright and morning star, but the other is the light of the world, O' I see, but do you Herald, yes I understand that Lucifer is the bright and morning star, and that the Messiah is the light of this world, yes exactly, then tell me why were you praying, why, why, why because I was trying to prevent Time and Life and God, to allow for these histories of the world to happen ever again, yes but by keeping it in darkness, no, by keeping the heavens within the light, that was up until the Angel Celeste sought to undo otherwise, but she was only trying to defend the Celestials, but this would never have affected the Celestials, as I am unaware why they would attempt to defy my authority, as it was left only to me to contain it, I never would have purposely affected the Celestials.

The only reason why the Heaven and the Earth were divided in the first instance, was because God favored Man over the Angels, but if Man is no more, then the Angels have succeeded in their obedience towards maintaining this the household of Heaven, and then peace and love would flourish and succeed throughout the universe, yes but what of Man, and what of him, I am not the custodian of Man, I am an Angel of the first and last formations, if Man is made to be contended with as a part of this creation, then the Messiah is his portion, and his portion alone, but what about the savior of the world and the light, could it be that you would prevent the restoration and the union of A New Heaven and a New Earth, listen well my Herald, for it is not in my power to prevent anything, only God can do that, however if my allegiances are forever to be tested, then I am forced to side with choosing that of my kind, the Angels of the Empyreans, I see, but do you see Haven, you who have been made and constructed to watch over his domain, and watch on as the wickedness of world is made to manifest, forever saving Man time and time again at the last moment from his own destruction, yes Nocturnus, but then at least tell me, as to whom were you appealing to when you were praying, was it Lucifer, no I was not, I was in fact praying to the greater part of myself, the other, then you mean that you were praying to Angelus E' Diurnāl yes, but why, to keep him sustained and to keep him at bay, to allow him to agree with me that this was the best way for all things concerned.

Nocturnus, please forgive me, as I am truly and deeply sorry, now is not the time for apologies my friend, as much as it is accepted, as you were not made to be aware of my intentions, and further yet the red rains have already come signaling the twilight has begun and a Messiah shall arise from out of its' ashes, and so it is too late to undo what has already been done, then at least come with me and let me return your eyesight for what has been done to you, nay Haven, let this prediction of punishment befit the crime, as does the end justifies the means, but you are not at fault here Nocturnus, nay I am not, but let this lesson serve as a true phenomenon, that I have always and eternally endured through the darkness of night, so that the light might flourish inside of me, yes, yes, I will let it be known that all however perfect, is not as it seems, and with that Haven had ascended beyond and into the Heavens above, leaving Angelus E' Nocturnus to wander betwixt the reddish mist and the beginnings of a new dawn and a new star arising.

All but once it had dawned upon Haven, that the observations of obedience was not mandatory or even demanded, as he now realized that it was a determinate choice of will, and not expected of anything or anyone, it just simply was a will that inadvertently led each one to take up his or her position or mantle, based upon the intentions that we have made to one another of any agreement and understanding, but as to why Nocturnus or even the Hayyoth had taken or even assigned and aligned themselves to take such extreme positions or roles of devotion, had demonstrated to him exactly how impartial this God was in his omnipotent wisdom and discernment in treating every soul according to its' intricate ways and inherent attributes, and yet it was also was, that this will of choice set upon the divine, also accounted for the promises of other possibilities that we somehow forbade ourselves, in having the ability to change our minds, or otherwise choose other such outcomes if needs be met.

Thinking of the trials endured and suffered by all, once the Herald had returned to the Heavens, so it was that the impact of the recent revelations weighed heavy upon his heart and mind, as he could neither see, nor find any optimum solution as he faced the complexities of the created of creation, and so upon entering once again, the Chamber of the Elect Few, and began to speak softly and thoughtfully in addressing all who were present, perhaps in our thinking or even in our speculations to figure the truth out, or to even come to any terms with any references in life, especially when faced with something so mystically significant as the resurrection, then surely we must all be unanimous in all of our agreements made, especially in accepting and acknowledging, that upon all accounts, that all are freely absolved of any misdeeds of a previous accord, so as to ensure that in our coming forth from the depths of the grave, and in returning back to the sanctum of life born out of the acceptance, that in our witnessing, that all at once is not as it mighten have been, for if only but once we are all to be transformed and renewed along with the renewal of all other things made possible, then this must also be the way of those declarations and promises of vestiges made long ago, which are now to become the invested way of the truth and the life.

No sooner than Haven had spoke, that all therein fell silent, and for a moment the Elect Few seem to weigh up and consider the true reality behind what had been said, as even the young Manoo within his eager and learned wisdom, did also find it hard to respond to such an enlightening statement, and so the silences endured further until one by one they all began to realize that nothing more could be said upon the matter, and yet none amongst them were even sure if they should now adjourn this Chamber, or reside and remain present, to thoughtfully sit through and consider its' implications, as it was no longer a question of what they could, or should not do as towards any preparations that should be made, but more of an expected reality, that suddenly the spirit of God would begin to move through the entire household of Heaven and that they in themselves would be caused to be moved and changed by the sheer influential force and magnitude of such a miraculous and eventful time.

Angelus Domini

INSPIRIT*ASPIRE*ESPRIT*INSPIRE

Chapter .XIV.

The Root of Death and Life

After these things I looked and behold a door standing open in Heaven and the first voice which I heard was like a (Trumpet!) speaking with me saying come up here and I will show you things which must take place after this. Immediately I was in the spirit and behold a throne set in Heaven and one sat on the throne and he who sat there was like a Jasper and a Sardius Stone in appearance, And there was a Rainbow around, In appearance like an Emerald.

Angelus Domini

The Root of Death and Life

I am the light of this world, and the world is in me, as you are also of the world, and the world is also inside of you, as we are all infinitely tied and knotted and together, and yet we are at a distance, in that we are as far as the eyes can see, and yet we are held together by the elements of our creation, and yet we are only born of flesh and blood, and yet we are contained by our bodily forms, and yet we are as far and as wide as the divinity of dreams, as much as we are the energies of spirits, and yet we are the mortals of physicality, as from before the creation of the world we did not know our perfect form before it existed, as the physical world only requires our mortal and physical form, but before creation, we are simply all of one form and of one body, as the Earth and the Sky are not separate, but have distinctive shape and form, and yet what is the difference, except that the eyes see and the soul responds, the spirit knows and the heart communicates, all are one, except that we agree to demonstrate distinctions between us and them, even as the world is full of our inhabitance, all souls are at varying degrees of infancy or maturity, as the living are constantly in a state of change, but the passing of the old, is constantly in a state of forming and molding itself back into the womb of the world, to have everything and nothing within every state of this our Equilibrium, is for the world to constantly change as much as it is evolving according through us as mortals, and yet as souls, as spirits, the world did not make itself, as much as we did not create it ourselves, but were brought into creation as much as the world was brought into its' own existence.

Life is Life, and Life is Death, and yet Life is Eternal and Death is only but temporary, and so to die is not the end of Life, but to change, as eternity is preparing for the end as much as it is in readiness for the beginning, for if we did not change, then we could not move in and out of each and every form our inherent and natural bodily functions, until we have arrived at a state and a stage where the renewed body is fully fit and functional for its' completion and fulfillment of purpose, as for the perfect form, which is to make the consciousness of the soul and the spirit to harmonize with itself until the resurrected body is fully restored and resourced in becoming compatible with the world, in order to be a part of the world that is created for and to sustain it, if we are to become new beings, then the world must also become renewed in order to maintain and benefit and befit us for our purposes, as much as we are dependent upon the elemental sustenance's for our energies, so too does a new form take on its' likeness up until it is fit for the purposes of it is intended for within its' environment, as the spirit of the body, is the final and complete state and stage, and yet so too must the world fulfill its' own spiritual purpose of environment in order to sustain and to maintain us, as the Spirit and the world must be compatible with one another, if the whole body is to be resurrected and made complete for its' new habitat in order to contain Life.

Have Faith in me, for I am faithfully yours, Have Hope in me, for I have Hope in you, Have Trust in me, for I am True to you, and I do not lead you to your Death and Destruction, but toward a greater awareness of the union of all things made worthy and worthwhile for you, as the Holy Spirit is here in the present, making sure and confirming that all is as I have said it is, in that God is at the heart of creation, and we are born of the creator, in being created, but as of yet, we are fulfilling the promises of the Christ and the Messiah, as much as we are new beings, so it is that Christ is also a new being, and so we must identify ourselves upon this expression and within the context of this newness, as we are yet to arrive and to come together upon this platform of understanding, which is why Faith and Hope and Trust have played such an important role in making all of our promises toward becoming fulfilled, as we cannot fulfill this ambition individually as separate beings, but an one unified spirit, which is the Christ like nature, which is inside each and every one of us.

For if everything were to remain presently as it were, then change would not allow us to fulfill these promises of the spirit, which is to take from it, the root, and the essential aspect of the personality and characteristics of a transformed, mind, body and soul, beginning with Love, Truth and God, as after we have fulfilled the basic requirements that Love and Truth and God, has taught us, only then can we begin to grow and develop and arrive at this new phase of our spiritual growth and fulfillment, inasmuch that we are all loved by Christ, in recognizing that the Messiah has perfected himself and his creation, in demonstrating to us, through Faith and Hope and Trust, that we can also achieve this state of perfection.

As much as you did not die but rather transitioned towards a state of perfectedness, as much as Christ the Messiah, also transitioned in duly laying down the foundations for the resurrection of the body, and so this renewed body, is not as it once was, except that it is now filled with and purified with the love and the spirit of Christ the Messiah, as this is how a unified world is made to manifest itself upon its' newly formed rebirth, in that now it is arisen, and so therefore all of the arising kindred souls have become likeminded, as all states and forms are now reborn along with this equal measure, and in possessing the same substance, which is in itself, the purity of Love, and the freedom of Truth, and the Godliness of the renewed spirit, as those of us who are awake, are now awakened and arisen in the spirit of the redeeming Christ.

As it once was, that in the beginning that the presence of God did move across the face of the Earth in order to create and sustain it, then so it is once again, that the Holy Spirit is also now made to move across the face of the Earth, in order to reignite and to reestablish new life forms, and a establish a new soul through the transformations of the spirit, as the formations of the first body was within its' infancy, coming forth from the pangs of birth, and did but momentarily live a temporary and mortal existence, whereas the second birth of the transformed body, is now complete in its' maturity, and is prepared for in its' readiness to fulfill an everlasting life of spiritual embodiment, as Life and Death are not of Equal measure, in that Life is eternal and Death is no more than a temporary aspect of Life, except that Death is only a part of the wholeness of Life, in order to fulfill the greatness of power that Life possesses in overcoming Death, so that an abundance of Life can become completely fulfilled and endured once more.

I now share with you this message of transcendence and of the transformation, if not only to mention of the metamorphosis of the spiritual kind, as all humankind are born of this, the same earthly organic materials that lends and gives itself over to transcendence, as it is within this interpretation and definition, that we are all maintained and accounted for beyond this, an ordinary existence, as much as we feel it, then so it is that we begin to know it until it is revealed, encompassing all from the root to the tip of salvation and put from far beyond the grave, for God has put and placed Christ the Messiah far beyond the ordinary perceptions of the material universe, as much as the spirit is seeking its' own redemption and deliverance beyond the simplicity of the physical universe, and yet all are still uniquely one, as each one, now begins to transcend from within this the ordinary existence toward this the now extraordinary Life and beyond, and yet in allowing for these promises, once made upon a bargaining that all whom are faithful and truthful, in being saved, are to be brought up from beyond the grave, with each one given over to the beginnings of a new Life that knows no boundaries and is no longer held down by the constraints of a former Life.

As much as the promises made by the Messiah in duly saying that whomsoever shall believe in me shall have everlasting Life, as in recognizing that Christ in himself has overcome and conquered Death, in order to release the body from the grave, so that all who are saved, shall be saved from a Life that would otherwise leave us held within the grips of Death, as it through the trials and knowledge's, that we begin to see and learn to journey between, what once and what now will be, as we should be aware that the second coming would only serve to suggest that there may even be a third, or even a forth, or even a fifth coming, but this however is insignificantly considered, and does not offer to support the true satisfaction of faith, that it was upon the first and only coming, that the Messiah, whom may have seemingly appeared to only have left us with a promise, as of yet to be fulfilled, did not prove so, but in truth Christ did not seek to leave or to abandon us, as upon his Death and resurrection, all of his promises were decidedly fulfilled, as we were even invited to bear witness, that Christ died so that we could have an everlasting Life in its' full abundance, and so the second coming is in fact the Messiahs invitation for us to come and to join with him, in becoming freed from Death, so that the announcement of this promise could be realized by one and all.

Inasmuch that the words spoken by the Messiah, are the words, not of Death, but of Life, as the word Messiah by its' own definition means the savior of Mankind, inasmuch as the risen Christ simply means the chosen one, as the one who was born to free us and to release us from the bonds and the strands of Death, Christ the Messiah, the Son of God, now ever present and with us always in the Holy Spirit, and presiding over the new heavens and the earthly kingdoms that is his rightful and just place amongst the stars and the household of Heaven, inasmuch that we do not know how or when we would die, or even how or when we were to be born, and yet in our trials and knowledge's we are made to be aware of the lives that we are now living, as such that we are between two states of consciousness, much before are born, and much more after we die, as much as when we fall and as much as we wake up, as it is put beyond our reach of understanding what exactly is taking shape and effect while we are asleep in Death, and how the awakening spirit is to arise upon the new day of resurrection and rebirth.

In finding out that through this one sacrificial bargaining and act alone, could serve to be the cause, and yet the result, and the fulfillment, that the savior of the world, would not only give us, but also grant us the ultimate opportunity of a lifetime, in becoming saved from the clutches of Death, in order for us not to fail and fall by the graveside, but instead to rise up, and in by doing so, to reap the rewards and the benefits of an everlasting Life, which takes also takes faith, and courage, and a belief of determination, that within these the last few and final moments when all is but lost, and when all has become desperate, and when all appears to down and defeated, that we, who have sacrificed nothing in such greater proportions, that we, who have lived with such unequivocal expectations, find out, that we have not been left out of receiving such a redemptive prize as this, in that the truth is ours, and the promise is kept, and that the savior of the world has sustained us in providing an eternal and guiding light, as the light of this world, so that we may safely seek out and find the passageway through to his resurrected kingdom upon the face of the Earth.

As the truth is evermore stranger than the fiction, and yet still affirms to present itself upon becoming the undeniable fact, a fact that no one could ever undermine or even fathom in calling into question, and yet here we are in finding ourselves accepting and believing other motives and other accounts of belief, that do not even measure up to, or go to serve or even to support any other such promises as set down and maintained except by this faith in Christ, as it seems that we would want to have it all, in acquiring this Life and the next, without so much as even examining, or truly knowing, or even recognizing as to whom we should accept and give ourselves over too in order to establish the true nature of this kingdom of Heaven, or is it that we find it too unbelievable or too amazing, or too farfetched, or too familiar, that we would discount it and overlook it, especially upon the final hour when it mattered to us the most, as none of us would choose to die if we knew that we could live, and no one here has decided that it is better to perish by the wayside than to exist, and yet such is the value of a Life without purpose or meaning, and such is the Life without Christ the Messiah, forever in your Life as the light of this world.

Open your eyes so that your soul may see, and so that your heart might declare it, and so that your spirit might rise, that in all the towns and cities, that there are each and every one of every kind of the churches and temples, erected and built towards the edifications of Christ the Messiah, if only as a testament on the subjects of creation, and so let me urge you to think and to consider it, if not upon the substantive measures that I have mentioned in saying it so, not only for my benefit, but upon the measure and balance that you have sought to seek it out and inquire after it, and examine it for yourself, as you will find in your doubtful experiences, that the is no other way other than this, in that God has permitted and allowed and accounted for each and every one of your experiences without charge, and so did not fail you upon your turning away within the darkest periods of your Life, if only for you to go and seek out, in finding the truth and the love and the gifts of God which are now being considered in your absence, so that should you find your way once again, that you shall awaken to find that you were not abandoned, albeit that perhaps upon your first account, you did not realize that you already possessed the keys to such a kingdom.

As it is not only the world alone that is made to be ready and prepared for this newness of transformation, but also for the souls that the spirit has lifted up and given over to a new life, as such it is that through Christ the Messiah, that everything is changed and is called by its' new name, as even upon the day of the resurrection, even Christ himself bears a new name, and so evidently comes forth with a new identity, as much as we are all called to bear witness and to give an account in our testimony, that indeed this has begun with a new sign of the changing times that is now taking place, inasmuch, that the former life has already passed away, ushering in a new day along with a new beginning.

Angelus Domini

INSPIRIT*ASPIRE*ESPRIT*INSPIRE

Chapter .13.14.

Angelus Domini

A **Tao. House** Product
Angel Babies Chapter.13.14.
INSPIRIT*ASPIRE*ESPRIT*INSPIRE
Valentine Fountain of Love Ministry
Info contact: ***tao.house@live.co.uk***
Copyright: Clive Alando Taylor 2019

Printed in the United States
By Bookmasters